P9-AOE-146

Diego's Buzzing Bee Adventure

by Alison Inches
illustrated by Ron Zalme

Ready-to-Read

Simon Spotlight/Nick Jr.
New York London Toronto Sydney

Based on the TV series *Go, Diego, Go!*™ as seen on Nick Jr.®

SIMON SPOTLIGHT
An imprint of Simon & Schuster Children's Publishing Division
1230 Avenue of the Americas, New York, New York 10020

Manufactured in the United States of America
First Edition
2 4 6 8 10 9 7 5 3 1
Library of Congress Cataloging-in-Publication Data
Inches, Alison.
Diego's buzzing bee adventure / by Alison Inches ; illustrated by Ron Zalme. —1st ed.
p. cm. — (Ready-to-Read)
"Based on the TV series Go, Diego, Go!(tm) as seen on Nick Jr."
ISBN-13: 978-1-4169-4776-9
ISBN-10: 1-4169-4776-0
I. Zalme, Ron. II. Go, Diego, go! (Television program) III. Title.
PZ7.I355Dhm 2008
2007006614

Hi! I am DIEGO.

This is BABY JAGUAR.

Do you see dark CLOUDS?

It looks like it will RAIN.

Quick!

We need to close the  .

WINDOW

We can stay dry inside.

I hear a buzzing sound.

An animal is in trouble!

What animal is it?

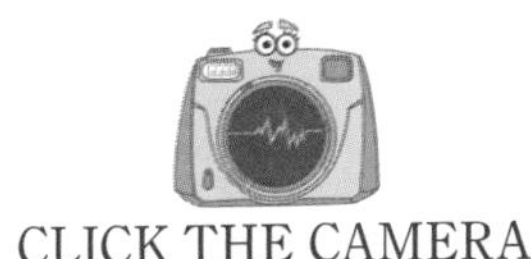

can help!

found a group of  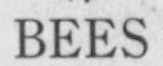

.

The BEES need to find a new home before the RAIN starts. BEES cannot fly in heavy RAIN. To the rescue!

Do you see the big  ROCK?

There it is!

The BEES are near

the big ROCK.

Do you see the BEES?

There they are!

The 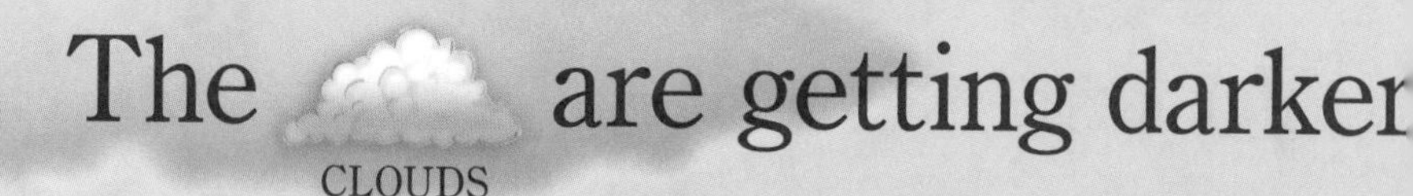 CLOUDS are getting darker.

We need to hurry!

Do not worry, BEES!

We will help you find

a new home!

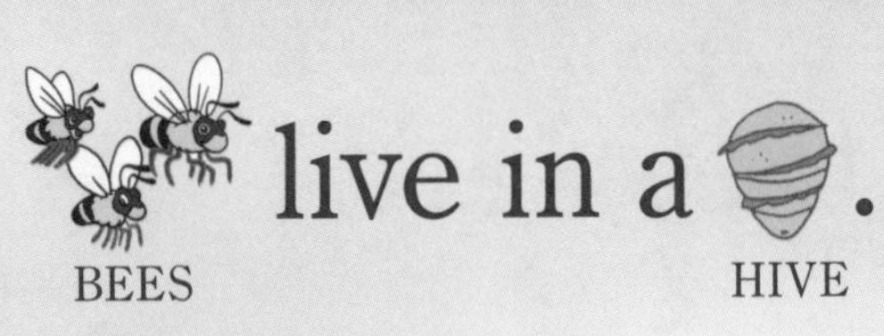

BEES live in a HIVE.

Help us find a good place

for a new HIVE!

The BEES say they need

a big HOLE for their HIVE.

We need to find a place

with a big HOLE.

Quick!

The RAIN is almost here!

This LOG has a big HOLE.

But a SNAKE lives here.

The LOG will keep the SNAKE dry.

We have to keep looking

for a HOLE for the BEES.

This  has a big  .

But a  lives here.

The  will keep the  dry.

We have to keep looking for a  for the  .

What about this TREE?

It has a big HOLE.

We need to look inside

the HOLE.

The HOLE is empty!

This TREE is a great place
for a HIVE!
It has a big HOLE
and no one else lives here.
The BEES can live here!

The RAIN has started!
We need to protect the BEES
from the RAIN.
RESCUE PACK can help us
protect the BEES!

What can we use

to protect the BEES?

An UMBRELLA!

Good job!

We will hold the 

over the 

.
Now we need to show the 

the way to the TREE.

Come on, BEES!

Follow us!

The BEES are going inside the TREE.

The BEES are safe!

We helped the BEES find a new home!
Now the BEES are warm and dry.

Now BABY JAGUAR and I need to get warm and dry too!

Thanks for helping!